FIVE LITTLE FIENDS

For my mum and my dad and
my brother, Stew

First published in Great Britain in 2001 by Bloomsbury Publishing Plc
38 Soho Square, London, W1D 3HB
This Paperback edition first published in 2002

Copyright © Sarah Dyer 2001
With many thanks to the BA Illustration Department, Kingston
The moral right of the author/illustrator has been asserted

A CIP catalogue record of this book is available from the British Library
ISBN 0 7475 5949 X

Printed in China by South China Printing Company
7 9 10 8

Five Little Fiends

SARAH DYER

BLOOMSBURY
CHILDREN'S
BOOKS

On a far away plain stood five lonely statues.

Inside each statue
lived a little fiend.

Every day they would come outside
to marvel at their surroundings.

One
day
they
each
decided
to
take
the
one
thing
they
liked
best.

One took the sun,

one took the land,

one took the sky,

one took the moon.

one took the sea,

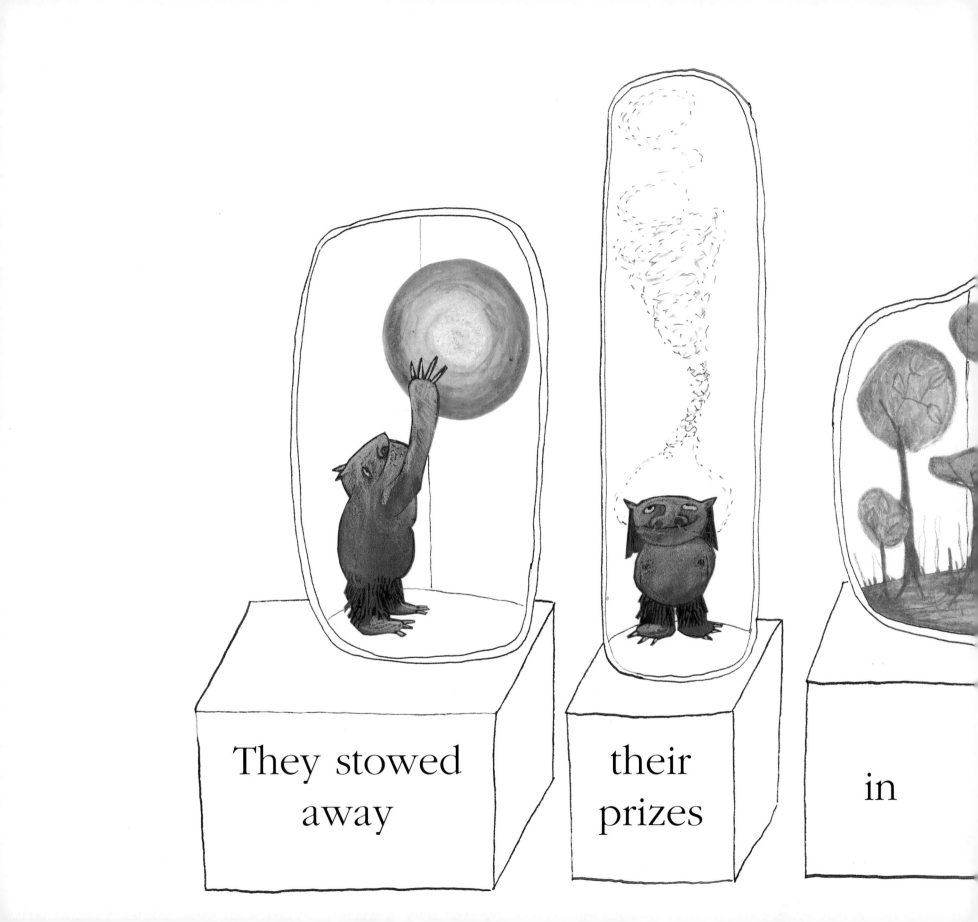

They stowed
away

their
prizes

in

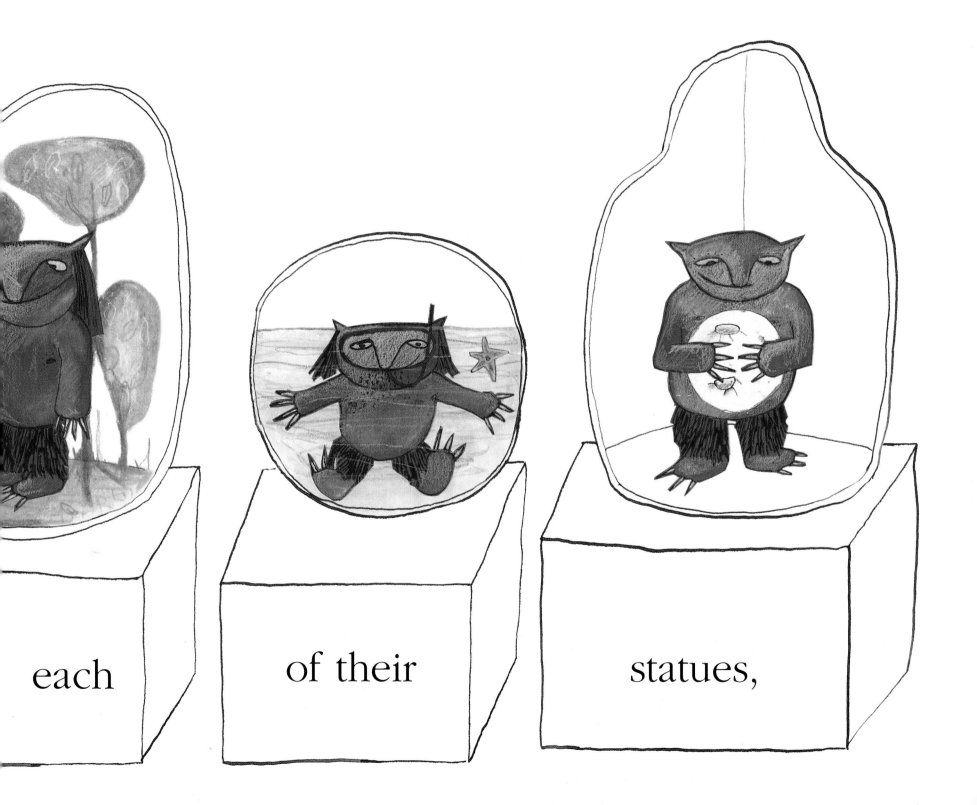

each   of their   statues,

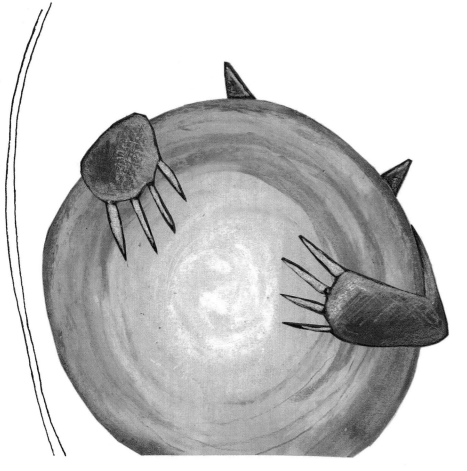

and admired them.

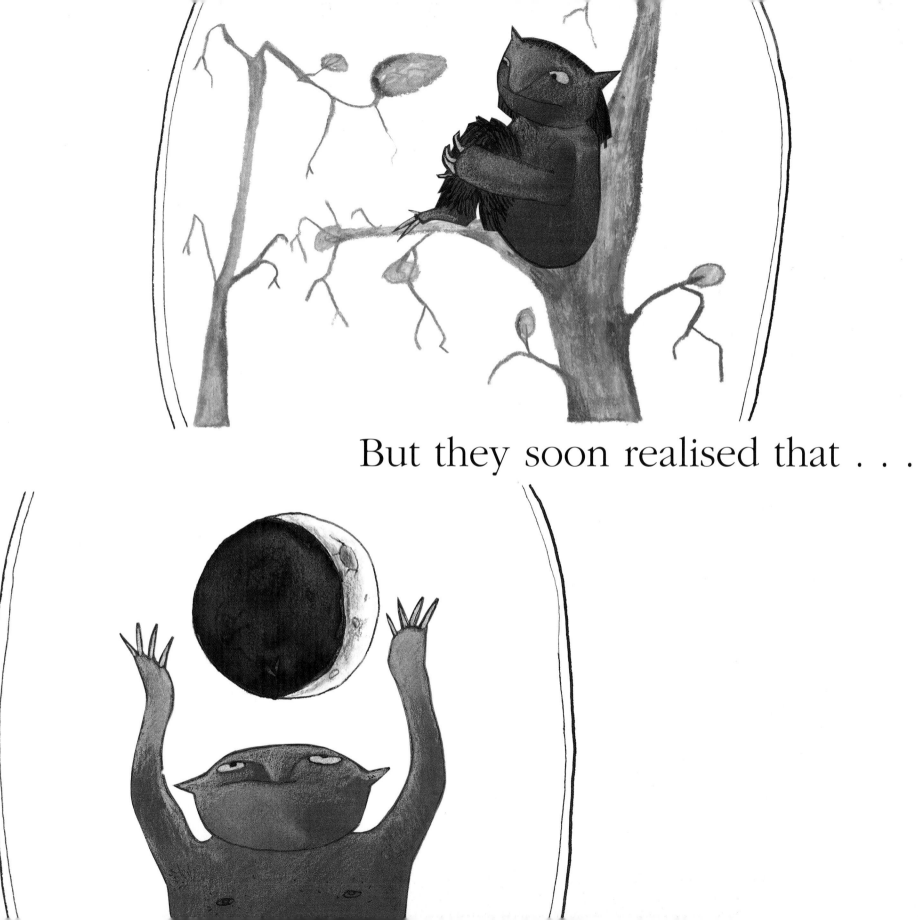

But they soon realised that . . .

. . . the sun could not stay up without the sky,

the
sky
was
nowhere
to
be
found
without
the
land,

the land started to die
without water from the sea,

the sea could not flow
without the pull of the moon,

and the moon could not glow
without the light from the sun.

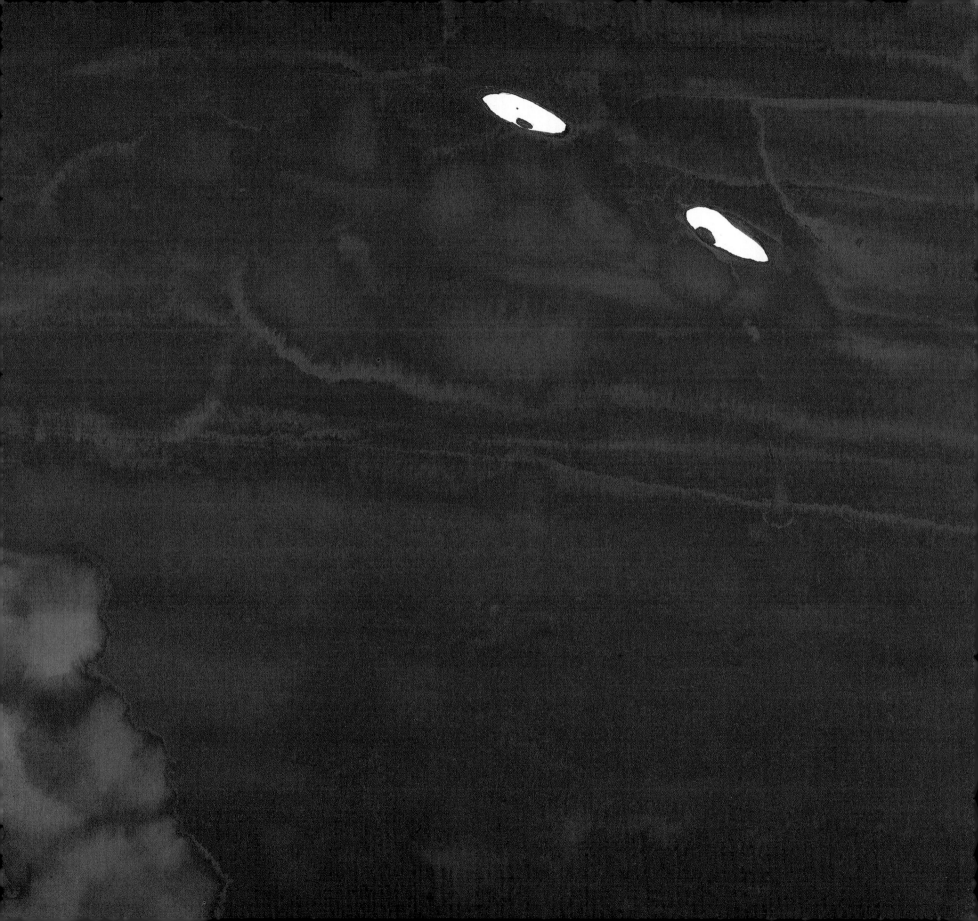

So they decided . . .

. . . to put everything back.

And once again marvel at their surroundings.

Acclaim for *Five Little Fiends*

'This is a truly original and wonderfully simple heart-warming picture book by a brand new illustrator who is just bursting onto the scene' ***Books For Keeps***

'The five monsters in this inventive and intriguing story will give children lots to think about' ***The Independent***

'An unsanctimonious ecological parable about greed and sharing for three-to-five-year-olds' ***Sunday Telegraph***